To my daughter Ona,
I love you no matter what.

Special thanks to Emily Ford and Becky Chilcott.

G.M.

First published 2021 by Macmillan Children's Books
an imprint of Pan Macmillan
The Smithson, 6 Briset Street, London EC1M 5NR
Associated companies throughout the world.
www.panmacmillan.com

ISBN: 978-1-0350-2391-2

Text and illustrations copyright © Gemma Merino 2021

The right of Gemma Merino to be identified as the author and illustrator
of this work has been asserted by her in accordance with the
Copyright, Designs and Patents Act 1988.

1 3 5 7 9 8 6 4 2

A CIP catalogue record for this book is available
from the British Library.

Printed in China.

Gemma Merino

THE **DRAGON**
WHO DIDN'T
LIKE FIRE

MACMILLAN CHILDREN'S BOOKS

Once upon a time,
there was a little dragon.

And this little dragon
didn't like fire.

She wanted to be a good dragon,
and make her dad proud.

But no matter how hard she tried,
she could not breathe fire.
Not even a tiny spark.

All that came out was . . .

. . . a whistle.

One morning, Dad took all his children to the lake
for a very important lesson.

"Your fire breathing is quite impressive," he said.
"But now there is something you must remember."

"NEVER, EVER go into the water.
It's cold, it's wet and it's HORRIBLE.
But worst of all, water puts out fire!"

As the years passed,
all the young dragons
grew their dragon wings.

All except the
little dragon.

She didn't mind not breathing fire,
she didn't like burning things.

But flying . . . she would love to fly.

So the little dragon decided
to build her own wings.

She would show her
dad what a clever
dragon she was.

But with her new wings she
couldn't do a loop-the-loop.
Or stay long up in the air.

Maybe she should try something else,
something more . . .

SPECTACULAR!

Ready,

steady . . .

BOOM!

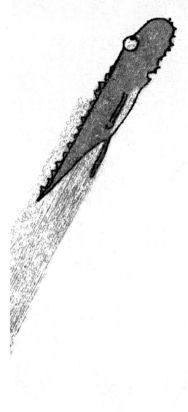

Now she was
flying higher
than anyone!

OH DEAR!

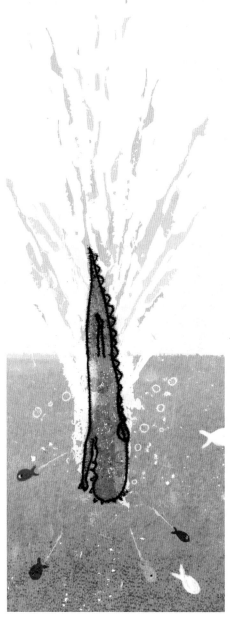

Her loop-the-loops were magnificent.

But she hadn't thought about the landing . . .

It was supposed to be cold.
It was supposed to be wet
and it was supposed to be
HORRIBLE.

But being in the water felt . . .

AMA

ZING!

It was refreshing.
It was fun
and it was better than flying!

Then, she saw something *incredible*.

There were other dragons in the water
and not one of them had wings!
"Oh, hello! Do you want to play?" they said.

But just before she could join in,
her dad saw her . . .

OH DEAR!

"I'm sorry, Dad. I didn't mean to go in the water but . . .
. . . I liked it!" sniffed the little dragon.

"And I'm sorry my wings haven't grown
and I *still* can't breathe fire for you.
Is there something wrong with me?"

And her dad smiled and said,
"No. Nothing at all."

"I don't mind if you can't breathe fire
and it doesn't matter if you don't grow wings."

"I think you are happy in the water
because it's where you truly belong.
You are not a dragon at all."

Then Dad took her back to the lake and said,
"You were born to dive and swim
and you can do things dragons can't do."

"But if I'm not a dragon,
then what am I?" she asked.

And Dad smiled and said . . .

"You are my wonderful *crocodile* daughter,
and I couldn't love you more."